BEHIND THE CURTAIN
Act Out History's BIGGEST Dramas

WHEN THE GROUND SHOOK

I0896416

SAN FRANCISCO EARTHQUAKE OF 1906

Virginia Loh-Hagan

45TH PARALLEL PRESS

Published in the United States of America by Cherry Lake Publishing
Ann Arbor, Michigan
www.cherrylakepublishing.com

Reading Adviser: Marla Conn, MS, Ed., Literacy specialist, Read-Ability Inc.
Cover Designer: Felicia Macheske

Photo Credits: © Everett Historical/Shutterstock.com, © hxdbzxy/Shutterstock.com, cover, 1; © Everett Historical/Shutterstock.com, 5, 6, 11, 12, 17, 18, 21, 22, 25, 29; © jenlo8/Shutterstock.com, 9

Graphic Elements Throughout: © Chipmunk131/Shutterstock.com; © Nowik Sylwia/Shutterstock.com; © Andrey_Popov/Shutterstock.com; © NadzeyaShanchuk/Shutterstock.com; © KathyGold/Shutterstock.com; © Black creator/Shutterstock.com; © Edvard Molnar/Shutterstock.com; © Elenadesign/Shutterstock.com; © estherpoon/Shutterstock.com

Copyright © 2020 by Cherry Lake Publishing
All rights reserved. No part of this book may be reproduced or utilized in any form or by any means without written permission from the publisher.

45th Parallel Press is an imprint of Cherry Lake Publishing.

Library of Congress Cataloging-in-Publication Data

Names: Loh-Hagan, Virginia, author.
Title: When the ground shook : San Francisco Earthquake of 1906 / by Virginia Loh-Hagan.
Other titles: San Francisco Earthquake of 1906
Description: Ann Arbor, Michigan : Cherry Lake Publishing, [2020]. | Series: Behind the curtain | Includes index.
Identifiers: LCCN 2019032889 (print) | LCCN 2019032890 (ebook) | ISBN 9781534159402 (hardcover) | ISBN 9781534161702 (paperback) | ISBN 9781534160552 (pdf) | ISBN 9781534162853 (ebook)
Subjects: LCSH: San Francisco Earthquake and Fire, Calif., 1906–Juvenile literature. | Earthquakes–California–San Francisco–History–20th century–Juvenile literature. | Fires–California–San Francisco–History–20th century–Juvenile literature. | San Francisco (Calif.)–History–20th century–Juvenile literature.
Classification: LCC F869.S357 L64 2020 (print) | LCC F869.S357 (ebook) | DDC 979.4/61051–dc23
LC record available at https://lccn.loc.gov/2019032889
LC ebook record available at https://lccn.loc.gov/2019032890

Cherry Lake Publishing would like to acknowledge the work of the Partnership for 21st Century Learning, a Network of Battelle for Kids. Please visit *http://www.battelleforkids.org/networks/p21* for more information.

Printed in the United States of America
Corporate Graphics

A Note on Dramatic Retellings

Participating in Readers Theater, or dramatic retellings, can greatly improve reading skills, especially fluency. The books in the **BEHIND THE CURTAIN** series give readers opportunities to learn about important historical events in a fun and engaging way. These books serve as a bridge to more complex texts. All the characters are real figures from history; however, their stories have been fictionalized. To learn more about the people and the events, check out the Viewpoints and Perspectives series and the Perspectives Library series, as the **BEHIND THE CURTAIN** books are aligned to these stories.

TABLE of CONTENTS

HISTORICAL BACKGROUND

San Francisco is a city in California. On April 18, 1906, it was hit by a big **earthquake**. The main shock lasted about 40 seconds. **Tremors** could be felt for hundreds of miles. This was one of the worst earthquakes in U.S. history.

After the earthquake came fires. The earthquake damaged gas lines, which caused over 30 big fires. The earthquake busted water pipes. Firemen didn't have water to fight fires. The fires burned for several days. They were finally put out when it rained.

Over 3,000 people died. Over 250,000 people lost their homes. Over 80 percent of the city was wiped out. Over 28,000 buildings were destroyed.

FLASH FACT!

The shaking ground opened up cracks in the cobblestone streets.

Vocabulary

earthquake (URTH-kwayk)
sudden, violent shaking of the ground

tremors (TREM-urz)
little shakes

FLASH FACT!

The fire that destroyed City Hall was called the "Ham and Eggs" fire.

Vocabulary

City Hall (SIT-ee HAWL) building where city government work is done

looting (LOOT-ing) stealing from shops or homes during a time of crisis

shelter (SHEL-tur) a place offering protection from bad weather or danger

City Hall was burned to the ground. All records inside were destroyed.

Things got crazy in the city. Soldiers came. They guarded the streets. They stopped people from **looting**. Soldiers guarded buildings like jails and banks. They helped provide food, clothes, and **shelter**. Over 4,000 troops helped.

San Francisco quickly recovered. City planners built a new and better city. There were new schools and hospitals. New businesses started. San Francisco was rebuilt by 1915. It was built in time for the 1915 world's fair. It became the city that rose from the ashes.

CAST of CHARACTERS

NARRATOR: person who helps tell the story

SOPHIE CHARLES: a 12-year-old girl who lives in Russian Hill, a neighborhood in San Francisco

PAPA: the father of Sophie Charles

MAMA: the mother of Sophie Charles

SOLDIER: a person who serves in the U.S. Army

CHUEN LEE: a young man who lives in Chinatown, San Francisco

JOHN MORRILL: a fireman who works for the San Francisco Fire Department

SAMUEL: a fireman who works with John Morrill

BACKSTORY
SPOTLIGHT BIOGRAPHY

Look Tin Eli lived from 1870 to 1919. He was born in Mendocino, California. In 1879, he went to China. He learned the Chinese language and culture. He tried to return to the United States in 1884. But he was kicked out because he was Chinese. He went to court. He won. The court said he was a U.S. citizen because of where he was born. Eli moved to San Francisco with his wife and children. He worked in a bank. The bank was destroyed by the 1906 earthquake and fires. Eli helped rebuild Chinatown. He got money from banks in China. He helped make Chinatown important. He designed buildings. He opened the first Chinese-owned bank in the United States. He got the city to allow fireworks for Chinese New Year.

FLASH FACT!

Chinatown features buildings designed in a traditional Chinese style.

ACT 1

NARRATOR: *It's April 18, 1906. It's early in the morning.* **SOPHIE CHARLES** *is with her* **PAPA** *and* **MAMA**. *She just turned 12 years old.*

SOPHIE: Papa, what's going on? What was that shaking?

PAPA: It is an earthquake, Sophie. It is a big one.

MAMA: Get under that table. Hold on to the legs.

SOPHIE: Why?

PAPA: We need to be safe. We have to drop, cover, and hold on.

SOPHIE: I can still feel the ground shaking.

PAPA: The earth is still **shifting**.

MAMA: We'll just stay here until the shaking stops.

NARRATOR: *The Charles family stays under the table. When they feel safe, they go outside. They live on a hill in San Francisco. They can see the city from their house. They check the damage in their neighborhood.*

Vocabulary
shifting (SHIFT-ing) moving

FLASH FACT!
This was the first large natural disaster to be photographed.

SOPHIE: There are bricks on the ground. And trees have been ripped from the earth.

MAMA: At least our neighbors are safe. And most of our houses are **intact**.

PAPA: Perhaps it's because we live on a hill and not on the land closer to the bay. That land was built up by dumping soil into **wetlands**. It's not very stable.

NARRATOR: *The Charles family looks down the hill. There's a black cloud over the city.*

SOPHIE: Oh no! There's smoke everywhere. I can see orange flames.

PAPA: It's really bad out there.

SOPHIE: What's that?

PAPA: That's a **cinder**. Get me some water! We need to put it out.

Vocabulary

intact (in-TAKT) in one piece

wetlands (WET-landz) lands consisting of marshes or swamps with moist soil

cinder (SIN-dur) a small piece of burnt wood that can still catch fire

FLASH FACT!

The residents of Russian Hill watched the fires burning the city.

NARRATOR: **CHUEN LEE** *lives in Chinatown. A* **SOLDIER** *bangs loudly at his door.*

SOLDIER: Open up! You have to **evacuate**!

CHUEN: I'm not leaving. This is my home. I've lived here for 15 years.

SOLDIER: You can't stay here. It's not safe!

CHUEN: You've been trying to kick the Chinese out of Chinatown for years. Chinatown is in the best part of the city. I'm not leaving.

SOLDIER: There was an earthquake!

CHUEN: I've survived other earthquakes. Even though that was a big earthquake, my house is still standing. I'll take my chances. I'm not going anywhere.

LOCATION SHOOTING

REAL-WORLD SETTING

Lotta's Fountain is in downtown San Francisco. The fountain is named for Lotta Crabtree. Crabtree was an actress. She paid for the fountain to be made. She did this in 1875. She gave it to the city as a gift. The fountain is made of iron. It's about 24 feet (7 meters) tall. Water comes out of lions' heads. Water flows during the day. During the 1906 earthquake, it was a special meeting place. People met there to look for loved ones. They met to share information. Since 1915, survivors of that earthquake have met at Lotta's Fountain. The last 2 survivors died in 2016. But people still meet there today. They go there to honor those lost in the earthquake. They meet at 5:12 a.m. on April 18. This is the time the earthquake started.

Vocabulary

evacuate (ih-VAK-yoo-ate)
to flee from danger

FLASH FACT!

Lotta's Fountain is San Francisco's oldest surviving monument.

SOLDIER: It's not just the earthquake. There are fires everywhere. You have to leave!

CHUEN: Fires? Are you trying to trick me?

SOLDIER: Open the door and see for yourself.

NARRATOR: *Chuen Lee opens the door. He looks in the distance.*

CHUEN: The fire looks like it's spreading.

SOLDIER: Buildings are falling. Grab what you can and run!

FLASH FACT!

Much of Chinatown was completely destroyed by the earthquake.

CHUEN: Where should I go?

SOLDIER: Get to the park. Follow the other people. Hurry!

NARRATOR: *The earthquake knocks* **JOHN MORRILL** *and fellow fireman* **SAMUEL** *out of their beds. John and Samuel live at the firehouse.*

JOHN: Earthquake! The building is falling down!

SAMUEL: This earthquake is nothing like I've ever felt before.

JOHN: I hear the bell going off. There must be fires all over the city. We have to go!

SAMUEL: We can't go down the pole. It's bent.

JOHN: Let's just **tumble** down the stairs. We have to go!

SAMUEL: I can't see very well. Dust and smoke are everywhere. I'm having a hard time breathing. This is terrible!

JOHN: Watch where you step. There are cracks on all the streets. There are falling bricks and rocks. There's so much **debris** on the ground!

SAMUEL: Look! There's a man over there. He's trapped under a door. He's bleeding!

JOHN: Let's pull him out. Drag him to a doorway. He'll be safe there.

NARRATOR: **JOHN MORRILL** *and* **SAMUEL** *try to help as many people as they can.*

JOHN: Help me **hitch** the horses to the fire wagon. We have to get to Chinatown. The fires are getting bad over there. We have to go get help!

Vocabulary

tumble (TUM-buhl) fall and roll

debris (duh-BREE) rubble from wreckage

hitch (HICH) to attach or fasten with ropes

FLASH FACT!

Firefighters used horses to quickly bring fire wagons to fires.

ACT 2

NARRATOR: *Firemen* **JOHN MORRILL** *and* **SAMUEL** *get to Chinatown. They try to connect their hoses to a* ***hydrant****.*

JOHN: There's no water in the hydrant!

SAMUEL: The water pipes have broken! The earthquake must have destroyed them.

JOHN: All we have is the water in our wagon's tank.

SAMUEL: I hear people in that building!

JOHN: Quick! Let's do what we can.

NARRATOR: JOHN MORRILL *and* **SAMUEL** *work as hard as they can. They rescue people. They put out fires. They haven't eaten or drank. They're tired. But they keep working.*

SAMUEL: The fire is getting too hot! We can't do much more here. We have to get out of here!

JOHN: There are other fires we can fight.

Vocabulary

hydrant (HYE-druhnt) an upright pipe used to draw water

FLASH FACT!

The Palace Hotel in downtown San Francisco was destroyed by fire after surviving the earthquake.

SAMUEL: With what? We don't have any water.

JOHN: We'll use dirt. We'll use sand. We have to keep fighting. We have to save our city!

NARRATOR: CHUEN LEE *is at a* ***refugee*** *camp. The city set up these camps in public parks. These areas are meant to house people who lost their homes in the fire. Chuen approaches a* **SOLDIER** *who guards the camp.*

CHUEN: Why are there only Chinese people here?

SOLDIER: This is a Chinese-only camp.

CHUEN: Even in disasters, we are still not equal.

SOLDIER: The law treats Chinese people differently right now. I don't think it's fair either. But it's the law.

CHUEN: Are you planning on taking Chinatown away from us? Is that why you brought us here?

Vocabulary

refugee (ref-yoo-JEE)
a person who flees from danger

FLASH FACT!

Many people had to stay in camps.

SOLDIER: Chinatown is burning. There won't be much left.

CHUEN: We will rebuild. Our leaders will make sure of it. We will make Chinatown better than ever! It'll be the star of San Francisco!

SOLDIER: I have to go. I heard City Hall just burned down. And people are roaming the streets and looting.

NARRATOR: ***SOPHIE CHARLES****, her* ***PAPA****, and her* ***MAMA*** *are still in their house on the hill.*

Vocabulary

dynamite (DYE-nuh-mite)
an explosive

FLASH FACT!

Citizens took what they could then fled.

SOPHIE: I just heard a loud boom. And I felt the ground shake. Was that another earthquake?

PAPA: No. That was **dynamite**. The firemen are blowing up a building.

SOPHIE: Why would they dynamite a building now? The building has survived the earthquake and fire. That doesn't make sense.

MAMA: They think it will keep another fire from starting.

PAPA: My friend is a fireman. His name is John. He told me firemen blow up buildings on purpose. They do this to create a **firebreak**. This is so flames can't pass. They're trying to control the fires.

SOPHIE: Papa, look more cinders! More sparks! They're drifting up from the city!

PAPA: Stamp it out with your feet!

MAMA: Look! Some of the cinders are landing on roofs and fences. They'll surely catch fire. That's not good.

PAPA: Quick! Get more water.

SOPHIE: From where? We don't have any more water in the house.

PAPA: Get it from the pond in the garden! We must stop the fires from getting to us.

BLOOPERS

HISTORICAL MISTAKES

Eugene Edward Schmitz was called "Handsome Gene." He lived from 1864 to 1928. He was born in San Francisco, California. He was a musician. He was the mayor of San Francisco during the 1906 earthquake. A mob boss got him elected. Schmitz was thought to be working for criminals. On the day of the earthquake, he made a mistake. He issued a proclamation. Proclamations are orders. Schmitz told cops to shoot looters on sight. He said, "[Officers] have been authorized by me to kill all persons found looting or in the commission of any other crime." This was against the law. He shouldn't have done this. In 1907, he was found guilty of taking money illegally. Schmitz went to jail. He ran for mayor twice again after that. He lost both times.

Vocabulary

firebreak (FIRE-brayk) an obstacle used to stop the spread of fire

FLASH FACT!

Gas pipes were destroyed. The gas caught on fire.

NARRATOR: *A* **SOLDIER** *arrives at the Charles's home.*

SOLDIER: I'm here to evacuate you.

PAPA: We're fighting the fires. They haven't reached us yet.

SOLDIER: The fires are spreading. For your safety, you need to leave.

PAPA: And what if we **refuse**?

SOLDIER: Then, you'll be jailed.

SOPHIE: Oh, Papa! We have to go. Let's just listen to him. I don't want us to be separated.

MAMA: Okay, we'll go.

PAPA: But I'll be back. I won't let my house burn down!

SOPHIE: Don't worry, Papa. We'll return and rebuild. The earthquake and fires may flatten our city. But we will rise.

Vocabulary

refuse (rih-FYOOZ) to not do something; to disobey

FLASH FACT!

Chinatown was later rebuilt from its ruins.

EVENT TIMELINE

- **April 18, 1906, at 5:12 a.m.:** An earthquake hits San Francisco, California. Fires quickly follow. The fire chief dies from injuries when the fire station building falls on him.
- **April 18, 1906, at 7:00 a.m.:** The first army troops arrive. They come to help evacuate citizens. People start to panic. They flee the city.
- **April 18, 1906, at 8:14 a.m.:** Big aftershocks hit. These are smaller earthquakes that follow a strong one. More buildings crumble.
- **April 19, 1906:** The governor of California arrives. The Secretary of War sends supplies. Prisoners are moved from city jail to Alcatraz. Alcatraz is a small island in San Francisco Bay. It has a jail from which it's hard to escape.
- **April 20, 1906:** The fire moves south. Over 20,000 people get on a ship to escape the city.
- **April 21, 1906:** Firemen stop some fires.
- **April 22, 1906:** The fire has stopped. President Theodore Roosevelt sends money to help the city. He didn't accept money from other countries. He wants to show that the United States could take care of its own problems.
- **April 23, 1906:** The governor tells a newspaper reporter, "The work of rebuilding San Francisco has commenced."
- **August 1906:** The California Street Cable Railroad Company repairs its building. It starts running cable cars again. Cable cars move along big wires.
- **April 18, 1907:** The Fairmont Hotel is rebuilt and has a grand opening party. It serves 600 pounds (272 kilograms) of turtle meat and 13,000 oysters.
- **October 19–23, 1909:** The city has built about 20,000 buildings. It hosts a three-day party to celebrate, called the Portola Festival.
- **March 28, 1912:** A new law is passed to rebuild City Hall.
- **February 20–December 4, 1915:** The city hosts the world's fair. The fair is called the Panama Pacific International Exposition. Exposition is a large public show.

CONSIDER THIS!

TAKE A POSITION! The 1906 San Francisco earthquake and fires have been called a disaster. During disasters, soldiers come to help. Sometimes, there's martial law. This means the military is in charge. They take control of things. Do you think martial law is good or bad in times of disasters? Argue your point with reasons and evidence.

SAY WHAT? Learn more about Angel Island. Explain how the 1906 San Francisco earthquake and Angel Island are connected.

THINK ABOUT IT! Are you prepared for an earthquake? Are you prepared for a fire? What would you do? Read about earthquake safety. Read about fire safety. Learn how to be ready for a disaster.

Learn More

James, Helen Foster, and Virginia Shin-Mui Loh. *Paper Son: Lee's Journey to America.* Ann Arbor, MI: Sleeping Bear Press, 2013.

Lusted, Marcia Amidon. *The San Francisco Earthquake of 1906.* Ann Arbor, MI: Cherry Lake Publishing, 2015.

Walsh, Kenneth C. H. *You Are There! San Francisco 1906.* Huntington Beach, CA: Teacher Created Materials, 2017.

INDEX

ABOUT THE AUTHOR

Dr. Virginia Loh-Hagan is an author, university professor, and former classroom teacher. She is the co-author of *Paper Son: Lee's Journey to America*, which was nominated for a California Young Reader Medal award. She loves San Francisco! She lives in San Diego with her very tall husband and very naughty dogs. To learn more about her, visit www.virginialoh.com.